ABOUT THE AUTHOR

Damien Escobar began playing the violin at the age of eight. With years of practice and an unwavering passion for performing, he and his brother formed the Emmy Award winning group, Nuttin' but Stringz. Together, the duo received many honors and gained recognition for being the most successful crossover violin groups in musical history.

As Nuttin' but Stringz, Damien performed on many different stages, but starring on Nickelodeon's "The Fresh Beat Band" and "Jack's Big Music Show," would introduce him to an entirely new and unforgettable fan base. Following his appearances, Damien soon recognized the positive influence he had on young music lovers. Recounting experiences from his childhood helped him develop "The Sound of Strings." An imaginative autobiography meant to entertain and inspire.

This book is dedicated to my children, Kaydence and Tyris; my niece, Kimora; and the women who started it all— my mother, Gloria and my aunt Gail. They are truly my inspirations.

"Ring! Ring! Ring!" The school bell rang. It was time for music class to begin. Music class was Damien's favorite part of the day. "This is going to be awesome!" he shouted as he hopped into his seat.

Today, Damien was finally going to get his hands on an instrument. "Oh yeah! Oh yeah!" he sang. And he danced around in his chair like there were ants in his pants.

2

"Class, quiet down!" said Ms. Ponder, the music teacher. "When I call your name, come get your instrument."

Spread out across the room were different kinds of instruments. The class had learned about them all.

The first instrument went to Kaydence. "BOOM! BOOM! BOOM!" With every boom, Damien's eyes grew wider.

"I can do that," he said to his neighbor as he watched Kaydence bang a few times on the drums.

Kimora's name was called next. She was assigned the piano.

As she ran her fingers over the keys, Damien couldn't help but wonder how he would look playing the piano.

He imagined himself sitting at the piano wearing a dark pair of shades.

While striking the keys, he'd sing, "La-Dee-Da-La-La!" He wasn't a very good singer, but it didn't matter. It all sounded like good music to his ears.

Just when he thought he could hear the crowd cheering "Damien! Damien!" the sound of Ms. Ponder's voice interrupted his daydream.

"Damien! Here's your violin" she said, pointing to a case on the floor.

"The violin? Aww man, this is lame!" he mumbled as he walked over to it.

When he went to reach for the dull case, something shiny caught his eye. It was a guitar his buddy Tyris was holding up high. "Tyris! I'll trade you," he called out.

It was hard to say no to Damien. He was a cool eight-year-old kid.

He had style like a rock star and he acted like one too. The only thing he was missing was a rock star guitar. So Tyris agreed and the two traded instruments.

Damien was about to rock out on the guitar
when Ms. Ponder came to end his fun.

"Damien, give Tyris back his guitar and
check out your own set of strings," she said
while removing the violin from the case.

"I think you made a mistake, Ms. P. You want me to play the violin? Why don't you give me, umm, the trumpet...or maybe the harmonica?"

But there was nothing he could say to change Ms. Ponder's mind. Damien was stuck with the violin.

"Violins aren't for kids like me," he thought.
But since he couldn't get his way, he had no
choice but to try to play. Without letting anyone
know, he tiptoed over to a quiet corner with his
violin and bow.

"EEEK-EEEK-EEEK!," like a frightened mouse, the strings began to squeak. "SCREECH! SCREECH! SCREECH!," like a car wheel his violin started to squeal.

Playing wasn't very easy. And by the end of class Damien didn't like the violin. He packed it up and took it home. In his room it stayed in one place... sitting in its case.

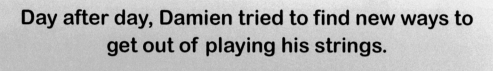

Day after day, Damien tried to find new ways to
get out of playing his strings.

"My chin hurts!"

"Left-handed people like me aren't
good at playing the violin."

"Come on Ms. P., the violin isn't for
kids like me!"

Every day he had a new excuse, but no excuse mattered to Ms. Ponder. After class she'd make him stay and together they'd play.

"Bum-bum-bum- bum... bum-bum-bum-bum!"
Again and again. "Bum-bum-bum-bum...
bum- bum-bum-bum!"

The more he practiced, the better he played. But no matter how good he got, Damien was too embarrassed to play in front of anyone else. "Violins are for dorks," he'd say.

Damien thought the violin was too fancy. And he sure didn't look like other violinist. As he played he pictured himself with slicked back hair, wearing a fancy-pants suit and bow tie.

"No, no, no, that's just not me," he said shaking his head.

"That's it, I'd rather quit!" So after practice
Damien decided he was going to leave his
violin behind. He slid his case under his
desk and when Ms. Ponder wasn't looking,
he quickly dashed out the door.

He had his weekend planned and it didn't involve his strings. He'd kick up his feet and watch TV, ride around on his bike, or even find a good book to read. "Tomorrow's going to be great!" Damien sang as he danced around in his tightie whities.

In the morning Damien was woken up by the sun. He jumped out of bed, ready to have some fun. He grabbed his helmet and wheels, and he yelled to his mother that he was going outside for a ride.

Waiting for the elevator, Damien heard a
familiar tune. Ding-ding-ding- ding...
Ding-ding-ding-ding" With each "ding" he
could have sworn he heard the sound of
strings. "I should have cleaned out my ears.
I'm hearing things!" he said to himself.

As he peddled down the street Damien heard a car going "beep-beep-beep-beep." And a bell from a church chiming,"ting-ting-ting-ting... ting-ting-ting-ting."

From the birds chirping in the trees to the mailman rattling his keys — even the train whistling by and a woman humming in a bakery while making a pie— everything sounded like his strings.

As he rode around his noisy New York neighborhood, all he could hear was the sweet sound of strings singing his song.

"Bum-bum-bum-bum... bum-bum-bum-bum!" And Damien began to miss his strings. He wished he could play along.

Damien couldn't wait to get back to school. And when the school doors opened, he rushed to his violin.

"Now I know what I'm going to do," he shouted. "New York City, I'm going to play a song you can rock to!"

Standing in the center of an empty room,
with his violin in hand, Damien began to jam.
First he played fast, it sounded like hip-hop.
"Bum-bum-bum- bum... bum-bum-bum-bum,
bum-bum-bum-bum... bum-bum-bum-bum."

Then he slowed it down to make music that
sounded like pop. He played high and low, fast
and slow. The sound of his strings flooded the
hallways. And one by one people came inside
the room to see his show.

Damien tapped his feet. He spun around. He closed his eyes and got caught up in the sound. Soon the room was filled with a mixed crowd who were waving their hands and stomping their feet. They all were dancing to Damien's beat!

Everyone clapped and cheered. No one laughed or
teased. Even Ms. Ponder was pleased. And from
that day forward Damien learned to be himself.
That's where it all begins! He was known as one
cool kid with a rock star violin.

Made in the USA
Middletown, DE
09 April 2017